# HANK BROOKS

# *Lustful* DESIRES

## Gay Romance

# WARNING

This book contains sexually explicit scenes and adult language. It may be considered offensive to some readers. This book is for sale to adults ONLY.

* * * * * * * * * * * * * * * * * * * *

Please store your files wisely where they cannot be accessed by underage readers.

Please feel free to send me an email. Just know that these emails are filtered by my publisher. Good news is always welcome.

Hank Brooks – **hank_brooks@awesomeauthors.org**

## About the Publisher

**4Fun Publishing,** a member of **BLVNP Incorporated**, 340 S. Lemon #6200, Walnut CA 91789, info@blvnp.com / legal@blvnp.com
NOTE: Due to the highly emotional reaction of some people to works of erotic fiction, any email sent to the above address that contains foul language or religious references is automatically deleted by our anti-spam software and will not be seen. All other communications are welcome.

## DISCLAIMER

Please don't be stupid and kill yourself. This book is a work of FICTION. Do not try any new sexual practice that you find in this book. It is fiction and not to be confused with reality. Neither the author nor the publisher or its associates assume any responsibility for any loss, injury, death or legal consequences resulting from acting on the contents in this book. Every character in this book is over 18 years of age. The author's opinions are not to be construed as the opinions of the publisher. The material in this book is for entertainment purposes ONLY. Enjoy.

# *Lustful Desires*

## Gay Romance

By: Hank Brooks

© Hank Brooks 2014

ISBN: 978-1-62761-729-1

My name is Cory Henderson. I am nineteen years young, and I am gay. Nobody knows that about me, except me. It doesn't really matter. The only sex I have is with myself. I am still a virgin.

Unlike most gay men, I am heavily into sports. I am a gymnast, which is what stereotypically one would expect a gay man (into sports) to be. I am on my college's gymnastic team. I am good, but not good enough to have Olympic aspirations. I suspect that at least one other member of my team is gay, but I am not entirely sure, and I am not about to come onto him. If he has any suspicions about me, I would imagine he feels the same way, and wouldn't dare to out himself to me. Anyhow, I have no sexual desires for him.

I am built like a typical gymnast. I am only five feet, eight inches tall, but my muscles have muscles. I am aware of the admiring glances of my fellow students, both male and female. Unfortunately, only my teammates have seen my cock, and only in the shower, and only in its flaccid state. It's a five-inch, cut beauty. It has some heft as well, and reaches about seven inches when I whack off.

So far I have had no problem curbing my sexual appetite, or living with my secret. There is only one area of my life that is giving me trouble. Late last August, when I met my roommate for the first time, I was consumed with lust. Ray Jensen is an athlete also, and he plays football with our college team. He is six feet, two inches tall. His skin color is a light mocha. His body is hairy, whereas I am almost hairless. I know that he is nearly as muscular as I am, but he weighs two hundred fifty pounds. His muscles are somewhat hidden by some flab.

It doesn't matter to me. The first time I saw him naked, I gasped out loud, and Ray laughed. He is uncut and his monstrous black cock, when flaccid, is as big as mine is, when erect. It is also twice as fat around. I saw it hard the first morning we roomed together, and I believe it was as big as a baseball bat. Perhaps I exaggerate, but it seemed that way to me.

Sometime during the first week of the semester, I came back to our room very late in the evening. The gym team had really been put through the ropes that afternoon. Ray was sound asleep, lying naked in his bed. His cover sheet was pushed down to the foot of his bed. He was flat on his back, and his monster was at full mast. I found out later that the football team had been put through an equally rigorous practice session. Ray had come home just a few minutes before me, and collapsed into bed.

He smelled fresh, and I realized his team must have showered before going home, just as mine had. I closed and locked our door and stood frozen, staring at him. I wanted desperately to stroke his cock with my tongue. I didn't believe I could even get his cockhead into my mouth. His luscious, dark purple head had fully unsheathed itself from his black foreskin, and it was facing the ceiling.

I approached his bed, and I swear I began to bend down toward his inviting rod. He smelled so good I almost swooned. Suddenly Ray groaned in his sleep, jolting me back to reality. I couldn't stand to look at his cock, so I took his cover sheet and draped it across his body. It didn't do much to hide the object of my lust. There was a fair sized pyramid outlined in the sheet.

As soon as he was covered, Ray mumbled, "Thanks, buddy."

Good God. He was awake. I shuddered at the thought of what might have happened if I had given into my lustful desires. I might be telling you this story from beyond the grave.

After that I did everything in my power to avoid seeing Ray undressed, but that was nearly impossible. We both slept naked, and more often than not, we ran into each other when we were showering in the morning.

One time, Ray asked me to wash his back. I needed to defuse my lust, so I laughed and said, "Sure, you want me to do your back so you can grab my cock." I laughed as hard as I could, and ran out of the shower.

While we were drying ourselves, Ray started to laugh also. "Sorry Buddy," he said, "I was serious back there, and for your information, I had no ulterior motive. Don't be so sensitive. I have no desire to get into your pants."

I wanted to say, "You can get into my pants any day of the week, big guy," but instead I said, "I'm sorry too. I guess I am too sensitive."

From that day on, I noted a subtle change in Ray. He still slept naked, but he was careful to remove his boxers after he got into bed, and he never seemed to shower at the same time that I did any more. Certainly I was glad about that, but the idea of his avoiding me while in the nude, disturbed me somehow.

Just before winter break, we were both lying in bed, talking about how much we were looking forward to going home. Both of us lived too far away to have gone home for the short Thanksgiving holiday. We had each packed a small suitcase and were going to share a cab to the bus depot immediately after our last class the next day. I don't remember it happening, but I fell asleep in the middle of our conversation. I usually pee before I go to bed, but I didn't that night. As a result I woke up about 2 AM.

I was about to step out of bed, and grab my robe to go to the bathroom, when I heard strange grunting noises coming from Ray's bed. I knew that sound well. Ray was whacking off. As badly as I needed to pee, I decided to wait until he was finished. I had no idea if he would be embarrassed or not if I caught him. I wondered how I would feel if he caught me going at it. I didn't get an answer from me.

I was trying desperately to get a peek at what was going on. There was enough moonlight coming into the room, that at the very least, shadows were discernible. I turned my head very slightly, and my efforts were rewarded. I distinctly saw a tube of lube on the bed stand between our two beds. Beyond that, Ray had his hand wrapped around his cock, and was stroking slowly. At least three inches of his cock protruded above his extra huge palm. Every so often Ray stopped stroking. After a short rest, he resumed. I realized that he was doing all he could to prolong his orgasm. That was well and good, but if I didn't pee soon, I was going to wet my bed.

Finally, I could bear it no longer. I pretended I couldn't see anything. I got out of bed, grabbed my robe and ran out of the room. When I got back, Ray was under his cover sheet and lying on his side. I didn't know if he had finished or if he had given up because of my intrusion. My question was answered about a half hour later.

After I peed, I was unable to fall asleep again. Ray must have thought otherwise. I heard him throw off his covers. I peeked at him through a barely opened single eye. He turned on his back, and continued where he left off when I got out of bed. I guess he wasn't greased enough, because he reached over for the tube of lube, and replenished the grease on his palm.

I continued to play possum. Eventually I heard Ray's stifled scream. I also thought I heard him mutter someone's name. I peeked and saw his fist in his mouth. I'd give anything to know whose name he called out. I wanted to know what lucky girl was the object of his masturbation fantasies.

After his jerking body calmed down, he reached under his pillow and took out some facial tissues. He cleaned himself as best he could. Finally, he got out of bed and threw his tissues in our trash can. He put the tube of lube into one of his dresser drawers. Grabbing his bathrobe, he left the room for a few minutes.

I don't know what devil possessed me while Ray was out of the room, but I decided to make him uncomfortable. When he came back, I sat up in bed and asked, "Are you OK, Ray?"

"You're awake?" he gasped.

"Yeah, I've been up since about 2 AM. I couldn't go back to sleep. What time is it now?"

"It's about four."

"Shit," I said, "get back in bed. Maybe we can get a couple more hours of sleep." I rolled over smiling, leaving him to wonder if I had caught him in the act of pleasuring himself. I sort of hoped he would ask, but he didn't. I rolled over and smiled. I actually fell asleep, and the next thing I knew it was 6:30 AM.

When I got up, Ray got up also. For the first time in a long time, we showered at the same time. For some reason, I wasn't afraid to stare at him, and I didn't care if he noticed or not.

After our last class, we returned to our room and picked up our suitcases. The cab we had hired was waiting outside. At the bus depot, we jumped out of the cab, waved at each other and went our separate ways.

The minute I turned my back on Ray, I missed him terribly. I hallucinated that we each dropped our suitcase, turned around, and started to run toward each other in slow motion. We never connected. We just kept running and running. The joy of going home for Christmas suddenly gave way to a deep despair.

When I saw my dad at the bus depot, some of my holiday cheer returned. He embraced me, nearly breaking my rib cage. Instead of feeling safe in his arms, I wondered how he would greet me if he knew that I was gay. If he was all right with that, I wondered how he would feel if he knew that I was lusting after a black man.

I celebrated Christmas surrounded by loving relatives and friends, but I continued to miss Ray terribly. At night, I fantasized that we were making wild love to each other. I dreamed that his baseball bat sized cock was up my ass, and it didn't hurt at all.

I tried really hard not to think about Ray. I realized that he was becoming an obsession with me, and it disturbed me. Things got worse. At about 5PM on Christmas Day, my cell phone rang. It was Ray. I panicked and ran upstairs to my bedroom so I could have some privacy.

"Hey Ray," I started, "to what do I owe the pleasure?"

"I really don't have to burden you with what's going on with me, but I thought you should know."

My first thought was that Ray was not coming back to school after the break. I panicked. "Tell me what?" I asked, afraid to hear the answer.

"I'm going back to school tomorrow morning."

"How come?"

"I've moved on, but nobody else at home has. I never knew my parents, Cory. My father was white, and he was a one night stand. My mother disappeared shortly after I was born. I was raised by her great aunt. When I got home, I found out that her son, my uncle, had to put her in a nursing home. He invited me to stay with him, but I would have to sleep on the sofa, which is more than a foot shorter than I am.

"I don't know if you know, Cory, but I'm going to school on a full football scholarship. All my old home friends are either still in high school, or just hanging out, unable to find jobs. They are still in gangs, doing drugs, and getting into trouble on a daily basis. Frankly, I have nothing in common with them anymore, nor do I want to resume their way of life, so I decided to go back to school."

"School doesn't start for another ten days," I reminded Ray. "Why don't you come here?"

"Thanks for the invitation, but I don't want to impose. No, I've made up my mind. I'm going back tomorrow morning. I've already changed my ticket. I just needed to let you know. So long, buddy and Happy New Year. I'll see you back at school."

Ray hung up leaving me speechless. Millions of thoughts were going through my mind. It was nice being home, but all my old friends had dates for New Year's Eve, and I didn't, nor did I want one. My folks were going to a party, and I had resigned myself to being a solo on New Year's Eve. I knew for a certainty, that the only person in the world I wanted to spend the holiday with was Ray.

Why did Ray feel the need to tell me that he was planning on going back to school? It was a weird thing to do. I wondered if the gentle giant wasn't reaching out to me. Did he feel about me, the way I felt about him? I decided that I was indulging in wishful thinking.

When I got downstairs, my dad asked me who that was.

"That was Ray Jensen, my roommate, the football hero," I answered with a lot of embellishment. "He was wondering when I was getting back to school. It seems that he is going back tomorrow. He has a date for New Year's Eve with one of the cheerleaders. She's a local girl, who lives off campus. She has a cousin visiting from out of town. She asked Ray to please get a date for her cousin, and he wondered if I would be back in school in time to take her out."

I was making this up as I went along, and I amazed even myself at my own inventiveness. My folks had never known me to date, and they were thrilled. The grin on my father's face was precious.

"What are you going to do?" he asked.

"I don't have a date here at home, so I think I'll go back early if you don't mind. Spring break will be here quicker than we know."

"Well, we're disappointed," Dad said. He always included my mother when he expressed one of his own emotions. I was glad she nodded to let me know that she agreed with him. "But I think you should go out with your friends also. You don't need to be sitting home alone on New Year's Eve."

"Thanks for being so understanding," I told my folks. "I think I'll go upstairs and pack. Can you drop me off at the bus depot on your way to work tomorrow morning, Dad?"

"Sure kiddo. Now you go do your thing. Honest, Cory, your mother and I don't mind cutting the umbilical cord at all." My dad was one in a million.

When I entered my room, I didn't know what to expect. Would Ray be there yet, or not? I hoped that I was the first to arrive. I really wanted to surprise him. I peeked in gingerly. Ray was not there. I looked in his closet. His suitcase wasn't there either. I sighed and started to put my stuff away, and then I stored my suitcase away. I got undressed and lay down on my bed. I hoped that Ray would arrive before dinner so that we could eat together. I knew I could never be intimate with him, so I settled for the joy of doing things with him, even as simple a thing as sharing a meal.

After a few minutes, I heard a key in the door. I hadn't locked it, and I was sure Ray would think that we forgot to secure it when we left. I pretended to be asleep, and I heard Ray gasp when he saw me, and then I heard him suppress a little sob. I heard him lock our door and put his stuff away. After he stored his suitcase, he too undressed and lay down on his bed … naked.

I looked over at him and he was looking at me. We smiled at each other.

"Why?" he asked.

It was a simple question, but it was my opening. I determined to tell Ray how I felt about him. I sat up and positioned myself at the edge of my bed facing him. "Ray," I began, "I'm gay, and I'm madly in love with you. I swear I'll never come on to you, or bother you in any way. Please promise me that we can still be roommates, and please, I beg you, stay my friend."

Ray jumped out of his bed and stared angrily down at me. I swear his cock had grown some. He was glaring at me, and I was truly frightened. "Damn you, Cory. Now you tell me, after all these months. If I had to go one more day without touching you, I would have gone crazy."

Grabbing me under my arms, he stood me up. He bent down and placed his lips on mine. If he wasn't holding me, I surely would have fallen. His mouth began to part, and I felt his tongue seeking entrance to my mouth. I was happy to oblige him.

When we had enough of dueling tongues, I made him sit down next to me.

"I need to know," I asked, "how long have you known you were gay?"

"All my life, I think."

"Me too."

"We're wasting too much time," he said. He pushed me gently down on the bed and started kissing me again. He didn't linger too long bathing my mouth. Soon he was kissing my ears, my neck, my nipples, and my innie. Suddenly he stopped.

"Let's do this in stages," he said. "It's your turn." I repeated everything he had done, and when I had sufficiently swathed his outie with my spittle, I crawled up to lie beside him. I placed my hand on his huge, hard as steel cock, and started to stroke. He started to do the same to me, but I had to stop him. I was too close to orgasm.

"Suck my cock," I begged.

"Yes, yes," he whispered. "I have been dreaming about this for months."

"Wait," I said, and twisted into a sixty-nine position. "I've waited a long time also."

I could get very little of his cock into my mouth, but I bathed his shaft up and down with my tongue, and stroked it with my palm. I managed to tongue his balls also, but his crack was out of my range. Neither of us wanted to cum, but we couldn't hold back. When Ray started to spurt, I caught his spunk in my mouth. I, of course, spurted down his throat.

Afterward, we lay side by side, kissing and fondling.

"You're very good," I said. "You must have had lots of experience."

Ray started to laugh. "You're my first," he said, "and you were wonderful. You must be the one with experience."

"You're my first also," I confessed.

Ray didn't answer. He just kissed me until I lost my breath.

"It's not true," I said to Ray.

"What's not true?"

"That you can live on love alone. I'm hungry. What say we get dressed and go into town for dinner? We've got a whole week to stay in bed and make love. The school cafeteria is closed, and we'll have to eat out a lot."

Over dinner Ray asked me if I would like to be his date for New Year's Eve.

"That depends," I answered. "Where are you going to take me? It better be some place nice."

"There's a gay bar in town I've heard of. Let's call and see if we can make a dinner reservation. If not we'll go after dinner."

"That's great. I've never been in a gay bar in my life."

"It's time for both of us don't you think?"

"Yes it is."

"And you know what else it's time for. It's time for us to fuck each other, but I need to stop at a drug store on the way home."

"Not for rubbers, I hope," I sounded sad.

"No dufus, for plenty of lube. Haven't you seen the size of me?"

"After we fuck each other, we're officially married," I pointed out.

"Then let's not waste any time."

I entered Ray first. I had done some reading and I thought I knew what to do. I greased up his ass hole and then my fingers. I inserted one finger at a time, and reamed him after each finger entered him. All he did was tell me how great it felt. Ray's ass hole was as big as the rest of him. When we guessed he was ready, I entered him doggie style. I didn't think there were other ways. That's how naïve I was, we both were. I went right in without resistance. I hardly felt anything and I told him so. Suddenly, I felt my cock being pressed from all sides. Ray told me that he was constricting his ass muscles.

"Now," he said, and I began to fuck. I was a novice and I didn't realize that I was stroking Ray's prostate. Before I even felt an orgasm starting, he was spurting onto the bed sheets. When he did, he constricted his ass even more, and in a short time, I came, screaming loudly, and spilling my seed in his bowels.

I lay on top of him totally spent. Neither one of us felt like starting another round just yet, and we both sensed it. I whispered in Ray's ear, "I want you to fuck me, but in the morning. It's going to be hard work, and I want to be rested so we can start the process."

Ray whispered back, "I love you. I don't want to hurt you."

"Don't worry, there's no way you can hurt me."

The next morning, we showered together, and played under the cascading water. We were virtually alone in the building. I told Ray to soap up his fingers really good and start to enter and stretch me. He got to three fingers, when I knew I would have to rest awhile. We finished showering, dressed and went out for breakfast. After breakfast we resumed our task in bed in our room. For nearly three hours Ray reamed and stretched me. At times I wanted to scream out in pain. At other times it felt so good, I didn't want him to stop.

Finally, after several tries, Ray greased my ass and his cock to an extreme and he started to enter me. Resistance, I am glad to say, was minimal, but the pain was maximal. Somehow, Ray got himself all the way in. His cock was crushing my prostate and the pain was leaving quickly. Suddenly, I felt so good. I thought I might be having a religious experience.

"Fuck me," I yelled, "and don't be gentle." By now Ray was so worked up, he came much too quickly, even before I could have an orgasm by prostate stimulation, as he had. I felt him softening and I was afraid he would fall out so I clamped down on him as he had done to me. He was so big that he stayed inside of me, even though he was soft. Eventually I squeezed and ejected him.

We were way too exhausted for lunch. We napped in each other's arms until evening, when we got up, showered and dressed.

"Let's go check out the gay bar where we are going on New Year's Eve," Ray said. "We can eat dinner there."

"We're both on school athletic teams," I reminded Ray. "Someone might recognize us." Ray broke out laughing.

"I know for a fact that half the football team is gay, or at the very least, bi. There is so much hanky-panky in the shower and the locker room, you would think we were at the gay baths. I'll bet there are more than a few brothers on the gymnastic team too. We won't find out tonight anyhow. They are all home for winter break." I decided that I would worry about being seen on another night.

The name of the bar was The Hot Spot. It was mostly frequented by students from the university, so the place was virtually empty that night. When we made our reservation for New Year's Eve, the reservationist told us that there were only two available spots after ours. I wondered if the students were coming back early, or if we would get to meet a lot of locals.

It was the first time in a gay environment for both of us. Of course, we got carded, and we were informed that we could have dinner, but we couldn't drink until we were twenty-one. I happened to mention to the waiter that maybe we should cancel our New Year reservations. He looked at us slyly, winked an eye, and said, "Don't worry. There will be plenty of guys over twenty-one who will order for you."

Based on the wink of a cute young waiter, we decided to honor our reservation. Whether we were lucky or not, depending on one's point of view, we met nobody there that night who we knew but we met a few great locals, and promised to keep in touch.

The school's first football game of the season had been scheduled for the Saturday before my first gymnastic competition during the fall semester. I had been there to cheer the team on at every home game. During the spring semester the team scrimmaged, but the season was over for them. They only had a so-so season, and as a freshman, Ray had played very little.

He returned the favor, and attended every match I was in at home, before and after our union. Life was good for us until spring break. I went home for Easter, but Ray elected to stay in school again. I was devastated. I couldn't let this happen during the summer months. I agonized what to do. As the semester was coming to a close, Ray had no place to go, and I wanted, no I needed, to take him home with me. That meant I had to come out, and then introduce Ray to my folks. I was scared to death. Ray insisted that he didn't have to go home with me. He said he would get a summer job and find a place to stay.

"Where?" I screamed, "In the streets?"

I started to cry almost all the time. In the end, I decided to tell half the truth, and see where it would lead to. I called my father and told him that my roommate was on a full football scholarship, and he had no home to go to except to a sofa in a slum apartment in a ghetto. I couldn't let that happen, and I begged Dad to allow him to spend the summer with us.

My father shocked me by agreeing immediately. "It's like that movie, The Blind Side, with Sandra Bullock," he said. "Who knows? Ray might be a pro someday. We should definitely help him."

The first hurdle was over. The next hurdle would be sleeping arrangements. We had a three bedroom home. My folks had the master bedroom suite of course, and I had the second bedroom. The third was set up as a TV room. Besides a big flat screen TV and other electronic equipment, the only other furniture in the room was a love seat and two lounge chairs. My father solved the problem before I had a chance to talk to him.

"You boys share a room at school," he told me. "You might as well share one at home. I found a very comfortable army cot in an army surplus store, and put it in your room."

"Thanks, Dad," I said with a little sob in my voice, knowing the cot would never be used. "You're a saint." I was jubilant. I threw my arms around Ray, and swore to come out to my folks before the summer was over. I made him swear also, but he was very reluctant.

We both found summer jobs at home, and contributed a small amount every week to our upkeep. Having a room to ourselves allowed us to make love often, but it was a strain not to be too noisy. As summer vacation came to an end, my resolve was renewed, but I was scared silly. My only solace was the fact that my folks genuinely liked Ray, and seemed to be color blind.

The night before our departure, I asked for a family conference, and that included Ray.

"What's up, Cory? You look scared to death. Why, you're all white," my father observed. He looked at Ray as if to apologize for using an adjective that might not be the best one he could have chosen. Ray was too scared to have noticed or cared.

I figured the best course of action would be to blurt it out. I was not one to beat around the bush anyway. Still I was terribly fearful. I had heard so many stories about young boys being kicked out of their homes and disowned when they came out. I made two fists, squeezed my eyes shut, and almost screamed out, "Mom, Dad, I'm gay."

"Yes," my dad said, "we know. We figured you would tell us when you met someone. I guess, you've met someone." He stared at Ray and smiled. He had second thoughts, and he said, "You are gay, aren't you, Ray?"

"Yes sir, Mr. Henderson, and I swear to you, I am madly in love with Cory. I'd want to die if anything ever happened to break us up."

"I guess we're your only family, Ray," Dad said. We'd like it if you would call us Mom and Dad." Dad said 'we' again, as always, and I looked at my mother to see if she felt the same way. She was smiling at both Ray and me, and I knew that she did.

The trip back to the university was a happy and celebratory one. It was the exact opposite of the fears we had experienced going home for the summer. Besides the fact that Ray and I could make love as often as our bodies and circumstances would permit, Ray now had a home, complete with a mother and a father.

Better than everything else, my lustful desires had become a permanent, indescribable reality.


### *The End*


Here is a sample from another story you may enjoy:

# HANK BROOKS

# SEDUCTIVE THOUGHTS

## GAY ROMANCE EROTICA

The first thing I noticed when I entered 'The Haven' was the absolutely beautiful entrance. I think they must have imported every flowering bush and tree from tropical Africa. Once I managed to get through the man made forest, fountains and waterfalls, there were certainly enough signs directing prospective buyers to the sales office.

At the moment, I was the only person there. Two eager sales people jumped up to greet me. One was a very handsome guy in his early forties. I wanted him to be my salesperson, but the woman beat him out. She was also very attractive, about twenty-eight or nine years old.

"Hi, I'm Nancy," she said extending her hand. I shook her hand, but for some ornery reason I didn't feel like giving her my name. I guess I was mad at her for denying me the pleasure of the handsome salesman. Nancy was not about to be defeated. She handed me a card to fill out. It requested the usual vital information, name, address and telephone number. Nancy won round one.

"Can you give me an idea of what you are looking for by way of housing? It would help me a great deal."

"I'm looking for a one story house, not too big, but on a big lot. I'm single and don't need a lot of space."

Nancy's face clouded over and I knew just what she was thinking. I told you. I'm a lawyer. I can read people's faces. Nancy was thinking, just like y'all, that single people are not serious buyers. She would have added an exclamation point to that if she knew I was gay.

I smiled sweetly at her and in my most sincere lawyer voice I said, "Nancy, let me assure you, I am a serious buyer." Nancy looked shocked. After all, I had just read her mind.

Let me cut to the chase. I ended up buying a ranch style three bedroom home, with a Florida room. It was on a cul-de-sac, so my lot was pie shaped. The front yard was not large, but the back was huge. I could even add a swimming pool to the back yard if I was so inclined. As an added attraction, the builder was able to save two huge shade trees at the back of my property, which gave me a little extra privacy.

Once he had my down payment, the builder seemed disinclined to rush completion of my house. But if you learn to be patient, you can get by. One day, almost nine months later, I took I ride out to 'The Haven' to check the status of my investment. Voila! The cul-de-sac would have five houses on it when completed, and all five were under construction. Six months after that date, I was the first of the five to move in to my new home.

It took me a few weeks just to unpack my boxes. The job was so overwhelming, that I just couldn't get going on it, so I set a goal of two boxes a day. Miraculously the number of boxes lying around began to diminish. The garbage service had advised me that they would not take corrugated boxes unless they were flattened. I flattened today's allotment of boxes and was schlepping them out to the curb for pick up, when a car drove up to the house on my right, and parked along the side walk. It was followed by a huge moving truck. Whoever these people were, they would be the second of the five cul-de-sac residents.

The wife was the first out of the car. She was about twenty-four or five years old. She was a dead ringer for the way Debbie Reynolds looked in 'Singin' in the Rain.' So you have an idea how cute and perky she was. The husband must have been occupied with something in the car because it took him a couple of minutes to get out of it. When he stepped out, I knew that I was in for big trouble. I could never live next door to someone so beautiful, and so sexy, and maintain my sanity. Let me describe him, although words are truly inadequate.

He stood six feet tall. He was wearing cut off shorts and a tank top shirt. The ripples on his chest rivaled the number of waves in the ocean. His biceps were huge, and bulged out indecently. His thighs and calves were so muscular that unless you looked twice, you would think he had piano legs, but then you realized it was all muscle. His brown hair was cut short in a buzz. Even from a distance, I could feel his sexy brown eyes giving me the once over. His nose was chiseled, his chin square, and he had a day's growth of beard. Ah, do you think that I did not check out his package? The shorts were old and worn, and the contour of his crotch was so evident that I had to will my erection away. Fuck, fuck, fuck! Why did he have to be straight?

When I was able to come down to earth, I saw that they were approaching me with the obvious intent of introducing themselves. I got myself together and started walking toward them. The woman spoke first.

"Hi," she said extending her hand. "My name is Marla DeAngelis, and my husband's name is Nicholas."

"Nick!" he corrected her curtly.

"Hi guys, my name is Eddie Gilbert. It's a pleasure to meet y'all." I shook Marla's hand and then reached for Nick's. His grip was so strong I thought he would break all the bones in my hand. He seemed oblivious to his strength.

"Wow," I said, "Are you a physical fitness instructor?"

"Yeah! How did you know? You must be psychic or something. I own my own gym on Ash Street. Marla here is an executive secretary for a big manufacturing company. What do you do?"

I heard the question, but my mind was so busy getting a membership in Nick's gym that I hesitated uncomfortably too long. Finally, back on earth, I said, "I'm a lawyer. Promise not to hate me." They both had the good grace to laugh.

"Where's your wife?" Marla asked, looking all around.

"Sorry," I said, "there is no Mrs. Gilbert. I'm single, but looking." Why did I say that? Marla would be sure to have me for dinner with every one of her single girlfriends. Dummy, dummy, dummy!

To change the subject, I asked, "While the guys are moving you in, would y'all like to come in and I'll make us something cold to drink?"

"Oh no thanks," Marla said. "I've got to show them where everything goes, but why don't you two guys get acquainted. Take Eddie up on his offer, Nick."

Nick seemed relieved of some terrible burden, and gladly accepted my invitation provided that the cold drink could be a beer. I assured him that his wish was granted and we went into the house, where I knew I would not be able to keep my hands off him. Please God, help a poor horny soul.

We sat at the kitchen table and I opened two bottles of Bud Light. Nick took one long swig, belched unceremoniously, and declared, "That sure tastes good on such a hot day. You gotta feel sorry for those poor sons of bitches hauling all my furniture."

He pushed his chair away from the table and sat on it with his legs stretched out. His short shorts were ever so revealing. The bastard wasn't wearing any underwear and I could see one of his balls peeking out. I am positive, in fact I'll bet you whatever, that he did that on purpose, because he was checking me checking him out. Do you know how hard I had to fight to keep from grabbing his crotch? I tell you, I was in agony. The worst thing is I believe he knew it, and he was showing me no mercy. My forehead was drenched in sweat, and my own shorts were bulging.

He certainly sensed my discomfort, because he put a look of concern on his face and asked me, "Is something wrong? You don't look so good."

I wasn't going to let him play with me like that so I simply said, "I'm fine."

Then he got bolder. He took a sip of the beer, holding the bottle with his left hand. As he swigged at the bottle head, he did two very suggestive things. First he laid his right hand on his enormous bulge, and second, after he took a swig, he began to lick the bottle head with his tongue like he was licking a cock head.

How thick could I have been? It would have been obvious to any casual observer that Nick was trying to seduce me. It should have been the other way around, but I was fighting the urge to do so. Still I couldn't be certain that I was right, and if I made a move on this colossus, it might be the last move I would ever make. Then he got even bolder…

If you enjoyed this sample then look for **Seductive Thoughts**.

**Also by this Author**

# **About the Author**

He was born many years ago in the small town of Brooklyn, NY. His childhood was not a happy one. He was overweight and terrible at all the street games the other kids played. By the time he got to Brooklyn College, he was all slimmed down and smart enough to avoid athletics.

Married at 21, the union produced three fantastic overachievers who subsequently produced five sons between them. He discovered he was gay at a later part of his life. He now lives with his fantastic partner, Leo, in Coconut Creek, Florida.

He has been writing gay stories for a good number of years now and has gained the support of a lot of fans from his written stories. He is also the writer of many more books published by this name, Hank Brooks on Amazon.

**From the Author**

Check my page on Amazon for Updates and interesting info.

Author Central - http://www.amazon.com/Hank-Brooks/e/B00CKI1Y1Y

If you enjoyed any of my books then please share the love and click like on my books in Amazon.

If you write me a review and send me an email I will send you a free book, or many. (Just know that these emails are filtered by my publisher.)

Good news is always welcome.

One Last Thing, For Kindle Readers...

When you turn the page, Kindle will give you the opportunity to rate this book and share your thoughts on Facebook and Twitter. If you enjoyed my writings, would you please take a few seconds to let your friends know about it? Because... when they enjoy they will be grateful to you and so will I.

Thank You!

**Hank Brooks**
hank_brooks@awesomeauthors.org